Edith Kunhardt

TRICK OR TREAT, DANNY!

Greenwillow Books, New York

Magic Markers and a black pen were used for the full-color art.
The text type is Avant Garde Gothic Book.

Printed in Hong Kong by South China Printing Co.
First Edition   10 9 8 7 6 5 4 3 2 1

Library of Congress Cataloging-in-Publication Data
Kunhardt, Edith.
Trick or treat, Danny!
Summary: Danny's parents and friends make sure he
has a happy Halloween even though a cold prevents
him from going trick-or-treating.
[1. Halloween—Fiction.   2. Sick—Fiction]   I. Title.
PZ7.K94905Dao 1988   [E]   87-14963
ISBN 0-688-07310-7   ISBN 0-688-07311-5 (lib. bdg.)

To Susan Hirschman,
Danny's fairy godmother,
with much gratitude

It is Halloween night.
Danny looks out the window.
He is sad.
He can't go out to trick or treat
because he has a cold.

It is dark outside.
The wind is blowing
through the branches.
The moon peeps out
from the clouds.

"What a bad, awful Halloween,"
Danny whispers.

"Come here, Danny, " calls his
mother from the kitchen.
"It's time to carve the pumpkin."

"First draw the face and
  make plenty of snaggly teeth,"
  says Danny's father.
"All right," says Danny.
  He draws a face with snaggly teeth.
  His mother cuts out the face.

Danny reaches into the pumpkin and scoops
out some slippery seeds with his hand.
"Yuck!" he says.
Then he scrapes the pumpkin's insides
with a big spoon.
His father puts a candle inside the pumpkin.

Danny carries it over to the window.

He walks very, very carefully.

"Now light the candle," he begs.

His father lights the candle

inside the pumpkin.

Then Danny sees something outside.
He sees a witch, a robber, and a ghost.

"Help!" he shouts. "Monsters!"

The monsters come closer
to the window.
Suddenly they snatch off
their masks!

They are Danny's friends,
Lucy, Mark, and Joshua.

They jump up and down.
They are saying something,
but Danny can't hear what it is.
Then he sees his friends run
to the door.

The door opens, and
three paper bags drop
onto the floor.
Danny's mother
picks up the bags.

"Hold it!" Danny's father calls.
"We have something for you."
He grabs a bowl from the table
and goes out the door.

Danny watches from the window
as his friends take candy
from the bowl.
Then, "Good-bye!" they call.

"Wait!" Danny cries.
He puts on his own mask and
puts his face near the window.
"Boo!" he roars.

Lucy, Mark, and Joshua
pretend to be scared.
Then they wave good-bye.
Danny waves back.

Danny opens the three
trick or treat bags. Inside
are candy corn, apples, raisins,
and some licorice witch's hats.
"Yum," he says.

"Speaking of yum," Danny's father says, "it's time for a cup of hot chocolate with marshmallows."

"And a witch's hat!" says Danny.

"What a perfect idea," says Danny's mother.

"For a perfect Halloween, after all,"
 says Danny.